BEDTIME
for
BEAR
by
BRETT
HELQUIST

HARPER
An Imprint of HarperCollinsPublishers

For Frank and Hank

Bedtime for Bear
Copyright © 2011 by Brett Helquist
Manufactured in China.
For information address HarperCollins
Children's Books, a division of HarperCollins Publishers,
10 East 53rd Street, New York, NY 10022.
www.harpercollinschildrens.com

Library of Congress Cataloging-in-Publication
Data is available.
ISBN 978-0-06-050205-8 (trade bdg.)
ISBN 978-0-06-050206-5 (lib. bdg.)

10 11 12 13 14 SCP 10 9 8 7 6 5 4 3 2 1
Typography by Mary Jane Callister
❖
First Edition

It was just after the first snowfall when Bear's
friends came running to his house.

Bear rolled over...

and tried to sleep.

But Bear heard his friends playing.

Bear grumbled and closed his eyes.

But Bear could still hear his friends laughing.

He could still hear his friends playing.

Bear opened the door.

Bear wasn't happy.

But then...

Bear tripped.

He flipped…

…and slipped…

...and tumbled down the hill.

Bear was wet.
He was covered in snow.
He was…

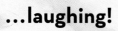

And they did.

Again.

And again.

And again.

There was snow to roll and stack.

There was snow to throw!

So down they slid.

And now it was getting dark.

It was bedtime for Bear.